Midnight Thoughts

Midnight Thoughts

An Anthology Published by Keres Publishing

Imprint: Independently published
First Edition – 2025

Published by
Keres Publishing
Email: kerespublishing@gmail.com

Cover Design: kerespublishing
Edited and Compiled by Keres Publishing Editorial Team

Dedication

Dedicated to the dreamers,

the night-thinkers,

and to every voice that dares to write,

even in silence.

This anthology would not have been possible without the dedication and creativity of our contributors.

We thank each writer for sharing their words, their emotions, and their Midnight Thoughts with us.

Special thanks to our early supporters who believed in this project.
Together, we have built not just a book, but a community of voices.

About Kerespublishing

For GenZ. By GenZ.
Keres Publishing is a student-run digital publishing house, founded with the vision of giving young writers and poets an affordable platform to share their words with the world.

We specialize in anthologies and debut author projects, offering opportunities for emerging voices to publish their work professionally and reach a global audience.

Through a blend of creativity, collaboration, and community-driven publishing, we aim to make literature accessible and inclusive for all.

For submissions, collaborations, or to learn more, reach us at:
✉ kerespublishing@gmail.com

Table of contents

Poems

Short story

Poems

A Talk

Author:

Navya Kumari

■ : softspells.140725@gmail.com

Instagram : @__softspells

Author bio :

Navya Kumari is a student and poet from Jaipur, India. Her work captures the emotional weight of everyday moments—those that slip by unnoticed but leave lasting impressions. Through themes of longing, transition, and quiet strength, she writes to understand the spaces between people, memories, and time. Her poetry is a soft echo of lived experience, shaped by reflection and a search for meaning.

A Talk

Were you ever in a desperate moment—
where you wanted to connect to a person
so badly that you forgot others' existence?
Well, I was.

Our memories are just a clutter of papers—
we haven't completely read,
yet, hold them close to our core.

Moments we had,
were desperate and sad,
spine chilling,
yet never felt cold.

Talks we never had,
feelings we just carried—
it's our memories, my friend,
that shape us in ways
we never or might ever imagine.

Illusion or reflection—
I don't know.
But we definitely saw something,
in ourselves and in others,
that flashed us.

Humans are interesting.
We are emotional, but desperate,
curative and creative,
passionate yet lazy—
and so much more to describe.

Still, no one ever knew you the best.
We might be under the illusion,
thinking we know ourselves best.
But do we?

Afterlife companion

Author:

Eshita Srivastava

■ : e.rivastava.writes@gmail.com

Instagram : @eyerivas

Author bio :

Hey People! I am Eshita Srivastava, a writer who wishes to let you escape from your sorrowness and hopelessness. Word is a weapon they say, I believe it's a key to the door which lets you free from any lock, any boundary.

Afterlife Companion

To feel the may, the gaze of a falling ray,
In between the leaves hanging on the branch,
Full of life, teaching how being alive looks like.

As I lie beneath it, with no breath,
No problem discussing it.
It throws a seed, like come on, it won't grow,
"To have hope," it repeats.

Reimburse the amount of thoughts hidden
underneath,
But how? My heart doesn't bleed.
Not anymore scream — it has been dead,
Buried under the oak tree,
With no tomb, no one around to meet.
The leaf sulks, saying it's just greed,
Enough guilt to not accept the greet.

"Of what?" my whispers swirled with flowing wind,
"Of me."

"We are besties."
"It never listens, does it?"
"You'll soon die too." It was a slip of doubt.
I wonder if it would've scratched
The part that has never been out.
But as the leaf said loud,
"That's what I meant — I'll join you,
You won't be there alone in loneliness."

Giving dead a hope
that one day,
Sun will meet the shore,
I won't find this place a bore.
I'll be truly free to rest.
Without a plan to conquer
The happiness hidden in the best.

As My Ship Sails

Author:

Naisha Kaur Sethi

■ : naisha.officialmail@gmail.com

Instagram : @merely_mymusings and

@_naisha.kaur

Author bio :

Naisha Kaur Sethi, a 16-year-old poetess and published author, writes with tenderness and unfiltered truth, often finding meaning in the quiet moments others overlook.For her, poetry isn't just words, it's a weapon, a war, and sometimes, a way through.

As My Ship Sails

Oh! it has been ages
Since I picked up a pen and got lost in the pages
Might be the first time I refused to write
The first time, when I didn't choose the light
So busy convincing myself everything was done
And all I could do was run,
From my own thoughts and emotions
I really tried escaping the commotion!
But it all came crashing down!
Once a fake smile, now just a frown,
Wondering where I lost myself?
Dust building on the memories I kept on the shelf,
For, I buried my emotions alive!
Dead but they continued to thrive
It's a full-fledged garden now
That keeps poking my heart somehow,
Did I mention they were thorns and not flowers?
Brutal cold nights and not spring showers?
All these thorns but still emptiness prevails

I keep missing the shore as my ship sails.

Cherishing The Things I Can’t Change Or Choose

Author:

Ziggy Wolff

■ : http://ziggywolffauthor.carrd.co/

Instagram : @ziggywlf.author

Author bio :

Ziggy Wolff is a lesbian & demigirl writer from Germany. She focuses on poetry, short stories and essays. The main themes are mental health, family issues, sapphic love, politics and healing. Ziggy uploads and shares her texts across multiple platforms, such as Substack and TikTok. Her work has a heavy essence of deep emotionality and cozy warmth.

Cherishing The Things I Can't Change Or Choose

I dwell in shadows,
uncertain of where I belong.
My existence is denied by the foul,
but oh, my heart longs for embracement.

All they can see is a blurred curtain;
They don't feel nor hear my plea.
Blinded by stereotypes, not aware
of what truly makes me, me.
For some of them, I'm good enough
when I'm naked with another.

Use and abuse, all for their own pleasure.
"Not good enough, disgusting!"
Their words always pierce deep,
no matter how often they'll repeat.
I'm faced by hundreds of dangers—
even stalked home by people
whose faces I have never seen before.

☾. Midnight Thoughts ☾.

I'm afraid I need to colonize a new planet
to live and love safely, freely.
In the shadows, I feel lost and alone;
craving understanding,
and finally have a place to call my home.

Fear clouds up my mind, I must admit,
but hope whispers softly—
teaching my hidden path
through the darkest of nights.

Grateful for her; for loving her,
as it's all that I can do.
The affection, the adoration, and the tension—
it's innocent, unholy, and spicy all at once.
So with every smile, every tender touch,
I embrace the truth of how much I love.
My soul's found in lesbianism; pride and peace,
in a world so far ruled and fired
by ignorant loath.

Closed Eye Scene

Author:

Navya Kumari

■ : softspells.140725@gmail.com

Instagram : @__softspells

Author bio :

Navya Kumari is a student and poet from Jaipur, India. Her work captures the emotional weight of everyday moments—those that slip by unnoticed but leave lasting impressions. Through themes of longing, transition, and quiet strength, she writes to understand the spaces between people, memories, and time. Her poetry is a soft echo of lived experience, shaped by reflection and a search for meaning.

Closed Eye Scene

Poet's note:

This poem reflects things that were never to be remembered, yet scared and raced your heart. There are moments and events that are hard to believe. Just like a nightmare, which feels unreal, something never happened before. They are flashbacks from the past or events we couldn't remember. Scary enough to give you a memory.

Emotions: silence and memories

Moral: Every past might not be fully forgotten, so if you recall it, don't panic.

☾. Midnight Thoughts ☾.

The broken memories
of the nightmare I had last night—
surreal and fearful,
yet never witnessed,
never imagined before.

I met a woman
with eyes like forgotten rain,
in a city that doesn't exist,
where clocks tick backwards
and everyone speaks in silence.

I was scared,
when I opened my eyes.
Reality was calm and safe.
But is it possible
to meet new people
and live through events
too strange to invent?

Something fresh,
so unfamiliar,

it feels like

a memory from

another life.

Cover girl

Author:

Navya Kumari

■ : softspells.140725@gmail.com

Instagram : @__softspells

Author bio :

Navya Kumari is a student and poet from Jaipur, India. Her work captures the emotional weight of everyday moments—those that slip by unnoticed but leave lasting impressions. Through themes of longing, transition, and quiet strength, she writes to understand the spaces between people, memories, and time. Her poetry is a soft echo of lived experience, shaped by reflection and a search for meaning.

Cover girl

Expectation stitched in borrowed words,
illusion wrapped in glossy expression.
Are we hanging—
or locked inside a cage made of emotion?

We tried,
we failed,
drifted like loose petals in waves,
rising, falling,
crashing while clashing
on this battlefield of becoming.

Were we ever the best versions of ourselves?
Or just paper dolls,
folded, edited—
shaped for those
who never cared
to read our story.

Echoes of Time

Author:

Soujanya Dodla

■ : soujanyadodla8@gmail.com

Instagram : @soujanya_dodla

Author bio :

Soujanya Dodla weaves emotions into words, capturing life's fleeting moments in poetry and prose. Writing, for her, is both expression and escape

Echoes of Time

My greatest fear is time—

Time whose motion erases the memories it carries,
time that reminds you you're no longer a child,

time whose neglect may breed chaos,
and time that brings the haunting fear of losing the
self you once were.

Time that cannot be borrowed when needed,
time that rushes when you are delighted,
and lingers when you are miserable.

Time, in whose embrace we find our fate.
Yet the beauty of time is this—
a river that flows, each second a gift,
a chance to create and recreate.

Time, a journey of growth, joy, and decline,
and in its fleeting light, we learn to cherish love

and seize each day.

Time—a dance of seconds, minutes, and hours,
each one a gift, breaking through.

So let us treasure time,
and make every moment count beyond compare.

Gate of faith

Author:

Eshita Srivastava

■ : e.rivastava.writes@gmail.com

Instagram : @eyerivas

Author bio :

Hey People! I am Eshita Srivastava, a writer who wishes to let you escape from your sorrowness and hopelessness. Word is a weapon they say, I believe it's a key to the door which lets you free from any lock, any boundary.

Gate of faith

Sometimes I wish to lose
Inside the moments, drowning away from the
momentum of curiosity.
Carrying burdens and profound struggle,
I learn, I seek experiences.

Well to be better than ever,
Indeed it sounds heavenly.
Wounds serve as bonds that carry such capacity —
The connectivity of hearts.

As it requires true efforts,
I summon the great depth of introspection,
To see and move forward,
Instrument dancing along the path of thrusts.

Do you feel the ending?!
Yes, we are near to the gate of faith,
Beloved by trust and wishes,
Upon the river of tears, carrying prayers and fears,

Beneath the sky of believers.

Life welcomes us, the people who believe in Noon
—
The power where the sun holds the hand of the
moon.
It takes us to the world where we can become the
one who understands
Own fear, desire, enlightenment, and tears.

To a better place,
Where we do not wish to give up ever soon.

I wonder

Author:

Eva George

■ : evageorge712@gmail.com

Instagram : @_.eva.george / @_.lilac.writes

Author bio :

An 18 year old trying to navigate through life in solitude, stitching her wounds with ink, hoping they might soak the ache. May these words meet you where you are most human, where you bruise, mend and pray for solace because sometimes the only way to hold yourself together is to let the ink spill what the heart can't say.

I wonder

I wonder if she jumps into the lake,
would they notice the stones in her pockets?

I wonder if they'd jump with her,
or just stand there, counting the ripples.

I wonder if the water's chill cuts deeper
than the emptiness she feels in her chest.

I wonder if the fish mistake her stillness
for something they can swallow whole.
I wonder if the surface will ever miss her,
or if the waves hold her like underwater ruins.

I wonder if the water remembers the weight of her,
or if it simply keeps on flowing, filling the space
where she sank.

If in the sentence

Author:

Eshita Srivastava

■ : e.rivastava.writes@gmail.com

Instagram : @eyerivas

Author bio :

Hey People! I am Eshita Srivastava, a writer who wishes to let you escape from your sorrowness and hopelessness. Word is a weapon they say, I believe it's a key to the door which lets you free from any lock, any boundary.

If in the sentence

If I extend my hands, will you hold them?
If I say yes, will you keep them?

My passion has been waiting on edge,
The night soon to dawn is seeing the end.

As I look up to the sky, clouds are wandering
Maybe to see me off.
I've heard they don't like people who dream high,
And as I am one of them,
I feel like I'm not belonging to any of the words.

If only I was brave enough to confront
The truth of this world,
I would look in front, aiming my voice up,
"I am not afraid to reach the sky," I would scream
loud,
Bursting my heart out.
Maybe they would have heard me,
Believe me,

Liked someone as brave as me.
But as the word 'IF' lies in my sentences,
I wish I could rewrite the destination —

To extend my hand to you,
Who's not here in the realm of knew.

Me of me

Author:

Eshita Srivastava

■ : e.rivastava.writes@gmail.com

Instagram : @eyerivas

Author bio :

Hey People! I am Eshita Srivastava, a writer who wishes to let you escape from your sorrowness and hopelessness. Word is a weapon they say, I believe it's a key to the door which lets you free from any lock, any boundary.

Me of me

Difference between me, and the one I ought to be,
So far, so much that I cannot imagine how to
describe,
The one I wanted you to greet.

Beautiful young woman in her late teens,
Glorious smile, long hair brushing her cheeks,
The me I wanted you to see,
Was a girl you deserved to with be,
As if destiny tied a knot for us to meet.

I kind of am disappointed,
That she was so far different from me.
She was a poem I wanted you to read,
Carved with blood and tears,
Not a forlorn poet like me.
I wonder if it's just my greed,
I've never been free from beliefs, from memories.

Being loved by you? It was so funny, you see.

The one I wanted you to love
Is somewhere buried in me.

Midnight thoughts

Author:

A.Sai Niharika

■ : arumuruniharika246@gmail.com

Instagram : @_unsaid._.words5

Author bio :

A passionate observer of life's quiet transformations,who finds poetry in everyday moments and heartfelt memories.

Midnight thoughts

Do you remember how you'd stare at the ceiling,
Lost in the colors swirling with pain..
Sometimes I wish I could slip back into times-
Where being a kid meant dreaming without fear,
Before anyone told us how heavy growing would
be.

I think about those safe nights, falling asleep into
my mothers arms-
God, that was the safest place I ever knew.
We rushed to grow up, didn't we?
We couldn't wait to leave home, to taste the
freedom, the independence,
And now… we return as guests,
Haunted by the echoes of our small selves
Waking up in the night,
Missing what we had- before we knew we'd miss it.

We hustle, we struggle, to make ends meet,
Realizing childhood's tiny denials were life's

sweetest treat.
I used to think she cared too much,
That her love was too tight, too close.
Now, some nights, I quietly wish
Someone would look after me that way again.

Is this what they mean about life?
How quickly everything changes-
How the ones who once loved their solitude now feels like hell
Maybe this is what growing up really is:
learning to hold yourself,
To face some things all alone-
But you do it anyway, finding comfort in small moments,
Carrying the weight with a little more grace each time.

And in all of it, maybe there's a strange kind of beauty-
In longing, in missing, in loving so fiercely
That you carry home inside you,

No matter how far you go

Midnight Thoughts

Author:

Naami_

■ : aniy7715@gmail.com

Instagram : _whispersoftheroad

Author bio :

I am new to writing, guided only by the heart. With no prior experience, I simply try to capture the feelings I experience while traveling and meeting people along the way.

If my words have mistakes, I hope they are seen as steps in my journey, not flaws.

Midnight thoughts

Midnight.
Once, I used to welcome it —
falling asleep early, without worry, without reason to fear.
Now, I lie awake,
needing the comfort of pills just to close my eyes.

This night…
it neither lets me rest
nor greets me with peace when I wake.
It carries the pain I hide in daylight —
the same pain that refuses to fade,
unchanged since the beginning.

They say pain lessens with time,
but mine only grows,
like the depth of an endless ocean
where no shore can be seen.

I feel myself drifting away from those I once called

my own,
until only the night remains beside me.
It speaks to me,
reminding me of every truth I try to forget,
showing me the faces behind the masks.

If light is hope,
then darkness is the shadow of hope broken —
the part that whispers
that life will never give you everything,
no matter how hard you try.

And so, I lie here,
with the night as my witness,
holding my truths,
and my unending ocean of silence.

Midnight Thoughts

Author:

Kk

■ : kourkhushpreet1926@gmail.com

Instagram : @_whispers_and_ink_

Author bio :

Kk is a budding poet and literature student, currently pursuing her BA in English Literature. Her work explores themes of love, loss, and healing through heartfelt verse. She writes to connect, heal, and inspire others through words.

Midnight Thoughts

It’s 3 AM and I’m still trying to sleep,
With tears in my eyes, I’m thinking deep.
We could have been — those moments, now past,
And promises made that couldn’t last.

We would have married, I’m sure of that,
A simple wedding, no need for the grand or fat.
A home, a family, just as we had thought,
A life full of joy that can’t be bought.

Now ifs and buts are all that stay,
No more we, just dreams that fade away.
I trace your name in midnight’s hue,
A silent ache for a love once true...

MY MIDNIGHT THOUGHTS

Author:

Tej

■ : jokerguy829@gmail.com

Instagram : inkedbytej

Author bio :

I belive that papers have more patience than people so I speak(write) with them and when i read i listen from tone of the writings

MY MIDNIGHT THOUGHTS

The clock whispers past twelve,
and the world slips into a softer shade of silence.
Shadows curl in the corners,
holding secrets the sun could never bear.

My thoughts drift like stray lanterns,
searching for shores they'll never reach.
I wonder if the moon listens,
or if she only pretends to care.

There's a quiet ache between heartbeats,
the kind that doesn't hurt,
but refuses to leave.
It wears the scent of someone
I can only find in dreams.

If night could speak,
she'd call me by the name I've forgotten—
the one you used,
soft as the space between stars.

So I sit here,
writing to no one,
and everyone,
hoping the darkness answers back.

Oh, to be someone's first!

Author:
not_a.poetess
■ : desaisaanvi08@gmail.com
Instagram : @not_a.poetess

Author bio :
I write poetries for him, more like in the memories of him.

Oh, to be someone's first!

Oh, to be someone's first!
to comfort me during my worst
one who would hear what I say
and never break my trust
Oh, to be someone's first!
to have someone to rely on
to have a bond so strong
a shoulder to cry on
and then my pain will be gone
a safe place to go
a safe place to grow
a safe place called 'home'
a place where I can hide
away from the evil sight
some where I can go and complain
and I'm not to blame
someone who'll understand
and not let it go in flames
some where I'm the first priority
and not at the bottom of the list

someone who will care
and I'll not just be the spare
a train where my seat is confirmed
and I'll not be at the station waiting on

Pages of me

Author:

Toshak

■ : makidiman786@gmail.com

Instagram : ashuetic_.palette

Author bio :

A man lost between his own thoughts and the world's silence, still trying to understand why.

Pretending to be strong I

how many days can I pretend,
Pretend to be something I never was?
They asked me—
I replied,
"A strong kid with ambition."

But I was always beneath the clouds,
Overshadowed, hiding,
Living in the shadows
Where no one could reach me.

As a kid,
I was always blank—
With only happiness lingering around.
But now, as an adult,
I wish I was guided the way I needed to be.

I thought of dying,
But even dying isn't something I could master.
Because they say

You need courage to kill yourself.

I was pampered, I was loved,
Yet I became the complete opposite
Of what they always dreamed.
They wanted a kid who'd bring home medals,
But I was the kid who brought home rants
About how I failed.

I was scared of failing—
Maybe my biggest fear.
But I couldn't say this,
So I said I'm scared of spiders and insects instead.

I was scared to face them,
So I fought with them,
I talked to them in ways that would make them hate me.
But they never did.
They loved me with all their hearts.

They still had hope,

That at least I could pass.
But as an ungrateful child,

I fulfilled the disaster—
I failed them.
I trembled their souls,
Made them cry.

But what could I even do?
I was so scared of failing,
That I stopped trying too.

Yet, I cried for everything I couldn't be,
And still tried to live
As I thought I should

But-

Pages of me
:A✓

But Maybe I just wanted to be heard II

I don’t wish to die,
I wish to live,
I wish to adore,
I wish to love.

But now I wish to vanish,
Because I was scared of failing.
I stopped wishing to try,
I stopped wishing for things,
I stopped wishing for him to live.

And I did stop…
But it took a piece of him—
A piece that shattered him.

But I don’t know if I mean it,
Or I just want this ache to stop.
I wanted someone to ask,
“Are you okay?”
But no one ever does.

I was never strong,
I just acted like I was.
I was never fine,
I just smiled like I was.

I kept losing,
And it became a habit.
I was scared of failing,
So I stopped trying too.

I thought stopping would save me,
But it took everything I had.

Now I'm left,
Only saying,
"I wish to die."

Pages of me
:A✓

Maybe I Do Like This Pain III

I wish to die,
But I've been having problems—
Problems that can never be solved,
Problems I can't escape,

Especially when all I want is to escape.
The nights feel cold,
My body feels heavy,
Like someone is clinging onto me,
Pulling me down,
Refusing to let go.

I've been having thoughts—
Thoughts of disguise,
Thoughts of disaster.
My mind feels like it's erupting,
Bursting into pieces I can't collect.

I see my lover—
Once so full of love for me—

Now in the arms of someone
Who never even praised her.
Maybe that's just how life is—
You lose what you love the most
To those who never deserved it.

I've been aching with thoughts,
Tremendous, suffocating thoughts.
They make me sweat,

They blank me out,
Like my soul leaves my body
For a few seconds—
And then the ache returns,
Heavier than before.

A companion once asked me,
"Do you like this pain?
Maybe i do—
Maybe this is the only peace I know now."
But I didn't know what to say.
Maybe they were right.

Maybe pain is the only thing
That feels like home.

This suffering,
This ache—
Is it really pain?
Or was it always just
Inside my mind
All along?
I don't know if it's pain or if my mind just needed a reason to suffer....

Pages of me
:A✓

I Don't Know the Ending Yet IV

Tbh, I don't know where this will end,
Or is it already the end?
Tears keep flowing down my eyes,
Like rain that forgot when to stop.

Life has become an absurd idea,
A routine of breathing but never living.
I'm chasing ghosts that once feared me,
Now I'm scared of my own reflection.

I don't trust people,
But I don't trust my thoughts either.
I don't know if this is the end—
Or just another pause,
Waiting to break me again.

Maybe I'll end it with an unfinished quote,
Or maybe I'll accept—

That what I am,

What I was,
And what I did,
Were just mistakes
That never got a chance to heal.

Pages of me—
But the ones written about me
Were burned
By the very people
Who claimed to love me.

Humans are optimistic,
But still, they make silly mistakes,
Like calling someone "forever"
And leaving them halfway.

I always thought
The end would be grand—
Like in books,
Like in films.
But maybe,
The real endings

Are quiet,

With no applause.

I don't know the ending yet,

But I do know

It won't be perfect.

It won't be loud.

It will just…

Be..

& Maybe this isn't the end.

Maybe this is the part

Where they stop reading..

Pages of me

:A✓

Relieved

Author:

Eva George

■ : evageorge712@gmail.com

Instagram : @_.eva.george / @_.lilac.writes

Author bio :

An 18 year old trying to navigate through life in solitude, stitching her wounds with ink, hoping they might soak the ache. May these words meet you where you are most human, where you bruise, mend and pray for solace because sometimes the only way to hold yourself together is to let the ink spill what the heart can't say.

Relieved

Just another night of brown teary eyes,
So frequent, it's become a routine.
Screaming out loud though only in her mind;
Every dawn the same old scene.

An aching heart like blazing fire;
Her shivering hands, not from the cold.
Yet still she smiles just the same,
The last lie that keeps her from going insane.
Those drowning eyes begging to be tamed,

To taste the kind of love she pours away.
But no glances near, nor arms to wipe her tears;
Just yesterdays relived as new todays.

The Last Truth

Author:

Sudhan Raj

■ : subashsaisudhanraju@gmail.com

Instagram : @sudhan_unscripted

Author bio :

Sudhan Raj is a poet who writes not to heal, but to bleed. His words are raw confessions of love, loss, and the silent wars we fight within. Every piece is a truth he never meant to hide.

The Last Truth

We were laughing,
Wild and free,
But then you said,
You had to tell me something secretly.

I never knew what was coming,
I could never bear that wave,
It struck me down,
A silent drown,
In a melancholy grave.

You said—
Everything I ever felt
Meant nothing in your view,
All my love was just of words,
Not a truth to you.

You said sorry,
I said I'm fine,
But deep inside,

That wound was mine.

The cut you left
Was oceans deep,
A pain too vast
For hearts to keep.

Guilt crushed you,
But pain crushed me,
And in the end—
We ceased to be.

Neither of us
Were as before,
Two lost souls,
With hearts at war.

Loving you was my only truth,
Dying inside was the price of it.

The Shimmering Grace

Author:

Aanchal Sikka

■ : aanchal0sikka@gmail.com

Instagram : @thewhimsymiss

Author bio :

Aanchal Sikka is just beginning her journey with poetry. Once a reluctant reader of poems, she's now discovering the joy of writing them, one verse at a time.

The Shimmering Grace

She ascends towards the lake,
Path adorned with flowers that sparkle.
Soft her steps, gentle her grace,
Even the sharpest thorns melt under.
Her payal produces a rhythm divine.
She doesn't know yet, but
She dazzles like sparkling water under the setting sun.

She takes her throne on a lakeside boulder,
Like a heavenly Apsara in the heavenly forest.
The breeze rushes to kiss her pink lips,
The water kisses her bejewelled feet.
The lotuses perform a graceful dance,
For they adore the one
That dazzles like sparkling water under the setting sun.

She leans a bit to look inside –
Who's the shimmering face looking back?

With innocent eyes, that are also wise.
A little bindi making her face bright,
Her Jhumkis sway, mingling with the breeze.
A beauty that makes time freeze.
She knows it’s her, and now she also knows
She dazzles like sparkling water under the setting sun.

A peaceful smile sits on her face.
Remembers a child with dull days,
How a brand new day was akin to a brand new fight.
A sad child, with nowhere to hide.
But how long can a child of God hurt?
The girl's mind burst with ideas divine,
So, she made her move, life took its time,
But now that mystical child
dazzles like the sparkling water under the setting sun.

She whispers her enchanting tale,
Fighting fear, catching it by its little tail...

To the mynah that sits on her lap,
The fishes in the water,
And the tiny titlis that decorate her hair with pink and blue flowers.
They listen with a curious trance.
Now they also know how she transformed into
The one who dazzles like sparkling water under the setting sun.

She begins her journey to leave –
The world awaits her divine grace.
The little adornments of the lakeside garden
Scrambled to take a last look,
For she seemed like the last light before an eternal nightfall.
She whispered a sweet goodbye,
Returned to the world, her fire blinding.
She had always dazzled like sparkling water under the setting sun.

The Snake Inside Me

Author:

Ruvaani

■ : gracewill92@gmail.com

Instagram : @ruvaani.unclaimed

Author bio :

Ruvaani is a poet and quote writer from Karnataka, India, with a BA in English, weaving timeless themes and raw emotion into original works that inspire, heal, and awaken.

The Snake Inside Me

The snake inside me keeps crawling,
up and down the spine of thought,
not venomous, not vile—just ancient,
coiled in silence, truth long forgot.

It slithers through shadows I've stitched
with threads of duty, fear, and grace,
its scales shimmer with borrowed light—
a stranger wearing my face.

It knows the rhythm of restraint,
the hymns of sacrifice unsung,
twisting through the hollow bounds
where once a wild girl hung.

She sheds her skin in quiet revolt,
layer by layer of not-quite-me,
each crack a whisper: "You're not this mask—
you're who you ache to be."

But still I bind her in soft silk lies,
of shoulds, of roles, of staying small.
And yet she rises—slow, unseen—
refusing not to crawl.

A sacred unrest coils in my chest,
dark, divine, and raw.
She isn't evil. She isn't wrong.
She's simply Nature's law.

And maybe one day I'll let her slip
into the world, unmasked, unbound—
the self I buried just to belong,
at last, no longer drowned.

The Thoughts of Midnight

Author:

Pratha Bang

■ : prathabang2010@gmail.com

Instagram : @theun_heardpoet

Author bio :

I am Pratha Bang. A enthusiastic student to write on various topics.

The Thoughts of Midnight

Midnight found silence around
But thoughts comes back in meri-go-round
Answer is waiting with surprise in it
Joy or sorrow are part of it
All the chaos scattered today
Is rethinked before next day
Building aim in imaginary dreams
Pending work with restless dreams
Caffeine is a myth making one awake
The passion of working can keep anyone awake
Let's make those hardwork ,memories of midnight
And resume your each dream from this point of
night
Midnight thoughts are your emotions
Flow from eyes and are not fictions
Be like river and do your function
Let's Break stones with infinite junctions

Warmth

Author:

Navya Kumari

■ : softspells.140725@gmail.com

Instagram : @__softspells

Author bio :

Navya Kumari is a student and poet from Jaipur, India. Her work captures the emotional weight of everyday moments—those that slip by unnoticed but leave lasting impressions. Through themes of longing, transition, and quiet strength, she writes to understand the spaces between people, memories, and time. Her poetry is a soft echo of lived experience, shaped by reflection and a search for meaning.

Warmth

Saw you in my darkness,
brightening up the room.
You were there in my
weak moments—
standing like a wall,
hugging me like my mom.

Forgotten whispers nowadays—
chatter like boiled-up gossip.
I heard them to get hurt,
yet you never left me,
stood by me,
sitting on that broken stool.

Thanks a lot, my love—
for brightening my life,
for sharing your warmth,
for removing my darkness,
for creating these—
unforgettable moments.

You accepted me as it is,
now it’s my turn to repay your love
with the desperate warmth—
I once required.

Who is she?

Author:

Sakshi Tiwari

■ : Sakshitiwari2885@gmail.com

Instagram : @nocturnal_.muse

Author bio :

I am Sakshi Tiwari a will be physiotherapist by profession and a poet by passion. I believe healing either by therapy or by words.

Who is she?

She is wild
Or just a child
But they say she is mature
Only she knows the pain not cured

You will always see her jolly
No one knows the tears prolly
She faced things that made her brave
Now…she just wants to hide in a cave

They say Problems make you strong, fight!
She just wanted to be safe not in fright…
But she is a star so bright ,
Fill joy in all, with her light.

She is gentle yet rough,
She is kind yet tough,
She is calm but chirpy,
All I know, she is worthy!

Little miss wants to do all at once
Does all by herself without any chance
She is simply a girl so rare
Who wants to live a life that's fair

I am Proud of this girl
Not too young not too old
Who fights through all, alone
And conquer the wars like she own.

Wine of Memories

Author:

Kalindi Kri

■ : kalindi1kri@gmail.com

Instagram : @lotus_lit1

Author bio :

Kalindi Kri is an international poet and writer. She's usually writing or thinking about writing. Insta: @lotus_lit1.

Wine of Memories

Oxygen scratches my throat
and forces me awake.

The moon sits at the bed's end
and watches over me.

But oh—
my nightmare sings me a lullaby.

I wake to their game
and ask for a glass—
forget to add water.

They reach out at the same time
and hand me something.

It's just a wine glass,
memories spilling over the brim.

I take a sip.

It has a cloying smell
and is sweet—

just like you.
Too good for me.

If only…
only I'd been less.
At least then
you'd have looked at me with pity.

The aftertaste is bitter.

I take a gulp.
Then another.
'Til the dark liquid is spilling
from the side of my lips
and running down my chin.

And oh—
my throat is burning.

☾. Midnight Thoughts ☾.

I wake in the middle of the night.

The moon is in the sky.

The nightmare is in my head.

Thoughts are at the end of the bed—

and I'm quenched.

Yet Another Heartbreak Poem

Author:

Megha Goswami

■ : meghagos14@gmail.com

Instagram : withlove.megha_

Author bio :

I love my coffee with one pump of overthinking and two spoons of existential panic. At 21 years old I am still discovering the world and all the joy it has to offer.

Yet Another Heartbreak Poem

Yes, she was happy but then she made her
sad (the other one's a girl too!) but it could
not be known at the time. Our condolences
for your accident. You can call anytime it's a 24/7
helpline—we are not ignoring your call
it's just so many people are on the verge
of suicide—giving up their life—we are hiring
if you would like to apply. The pay is peanuts
let's not drag the economy here.

Yes. The accident. What a broken heart.
Some pieces are back at the scene of the crash.
The medic could only grab so many
chunks. What a clichéd metaphor. How long
do I have to stick with it. For all of it? Fuck.
The heart has been stitched back now. No
vital chunks missing. Do you feel like killing
yourself again? Sorry we need to ask this
before we let you leave. Feel free to lie
we really need your bed. It's fine it seems

the self-destructing piece was left out
in the mending. That is some miracle! Sign here
and here. You will be rolled out. The pulse
missing.

Short stories

I love you, Buddy.

Author:

Ziggy Wolff

■ : http://ziggywolffauthor.carrd.co/

Instagram : @ziggywlf.author

Author bio :

Ziggy Wolff is a lesbian & demigirl writer from Germany. She focuses on poetry, short stories and essays. The main themes are mental health, family issues, sapphic love, politics and healing. Ziggy uploads and shares her texts across multiple platforms, such as Substack and TikTok. Her work has a heavy essence of deep emotionality and cozy warmth.

I love you, Buddy.

I was sitting on the floor, my legs cradled into my arms, while tears streamed down my face."Please, stay with me, I don't want you to leave," I pressed out into the dark shadow of the moonlight.
His claws tipped against the floor before he found a place to rest in front of me."I'm sorry, Amber, I can't stretch it out any longer," he said and laid his paw against my arm.He's a dog, but he talked to me. I couldn‘t remember a time he ever did, but I also couldn't remember a time he didn't talk to me. Is that a weird thing? It didn‘t scare me at least, it felt normal… comforting, even.

"But I can't do this without you," my voice began to tremble, the tears on my cheeks and chin slowly dried out.
He pushed his weight on my legs when he tried to stand upwards on his back paws. I took it as a sign to rest my legs down and let him cuddle into my lap.

"It's going to be okay, Amber, I will look after you," he said and slowly laid his little head against my chest.
"But will I see you again?"
"You will, but please take all your time, I need to see you reach your goals."

I could barely hold it together. I tried to keep myself under control, but knowing what was going to happen, what he wanted to happen, silenced every single beat of my heart. It felt as if someone were to steal my other half and I would never get it back — be destined to live forever with a big hole inside of me, a hole that would drag me into lonely misery for the rest of my life.
"Buddy, you will be gone…"
"Not in your heart," he looked up at me with the saddest yet most peaceful puppy eyes I had ever seen.
"When I'm gone, let me be your reason, I will miss you."
I couldn't imagine a life without him, I didn't want

to, but I knew he was right.
"If you really need to, please make it calm, Winston. Do nothing else but leave us in your sleep, okay?"

The second my lips shut, tears were streaming down my face as if a volcano just burst out.I held him tightly, hid my hands inside his fur and pressed his whole body against mine.
"I promise we will meet again, please take care of mom," he whispered against my neck, his nose pointed against my skin.
"I will try, I love you, Winston," I winced into his fur.
"Goodbye, Amber" he said and vanished into nothing, like a ghost, suddenly nothing was left between my arms, but the warmest and brightest beam of moonlight that I had ever seen.
I was shaking from head to toe when I heard a loud bark and claws scratching on the floor – it was the next day. I had been sleeping, and I remembered he was already gone for over a year.

Dear everyone

Author:

Shambhavani

■ : ssrajnarine.writersarchive@gmail.com

Instagram : ssr.writers_archive

Author bio :

I am 19 year old writer from the Caribbean, with a mission to spread love and comfort by giving others a voice to express themselves, through my work, in hopes that it helps heal even a little part of them. I hope to provide comfort or a safe place in this bustling world, moving too quick to say "it'll be okay" to each other. And I want whoever reads this to know that it will be okay.

Dear everyone

So many of us forget to give ourselves grace during the hard times, the lows of life. We forget that we too are humans. We too are allowed to feel the emotions as they come—within our own limits and our own space. We are allowed to not be okay too.

We abandon ourselves in our strive for success, our mission to help others, a duty to the world around us, a will to make a living. We downplay our wins when the losses become heavy. We forget that we are people in this world who—just like everyone else—feels emotions.
It's okay for the world to feel like it's closing in on you and like you don't know what to do or where to go. And it's okay to be scared, to be paralyzed by it. But you can't let it keep you there forever. You can't let it get the best of you.

It's okay to slow down sometimes. In fact, I think we all need to slow down a bit. Take a stroll instead of running, read a book instead of scrolling, have face to face conversations instead of phone calls, take a vacation even if it's a day.

Give yourself space to just be. To just exist. Not always attaching meaning or titles and labels to your existence. Just let it go, let it be. Even just for a minute. Don't attach explanations and identities like they're bullets disguised as trophies.
Dear moms, it's okay to feel exhausted and frustrated.
Dear dads, it's okay to feel overwhelmed.
Dear daughters, it's okay to feel angry and overlooked.
Dear sons, it's okay to feel burdened by expectations.

Dear everyone, it's okay. It's okay to feel. It's what makes you human.

Acknowledgment

To every poet who trusted us with their words—thank you. Midnight Thoughts exists because of your honesty, vulnerability, and creativity.

A heartfelt thanks to our supporters who helped shape this anthology into reality. And to our readers—you give life to these words with every page you turn.

To Readers

The midnight hour is where thoughts soften into whispers and truths rise unfiltered.

We hope these poems resonate with you, comfort you, and remind you that you're never truly alone. If this book touched your heart, please share your reflections with us and leave a review—it means more than you know.

Colophon

This anthology was published digitally and in print by KeresPublishing, a student-run publishing house dedicated to uplifting young voices.

Printed in India.
First Edition, 2025.

www.ingramcontent.com/pod-product-compliance
Ingram Content Group UK Ltd.
Pitfield, Milton Keynes, MK11 3LW, UK
UKHW040037200726
13845UKWH00054B/421

9 789334 43279